A BAN...

THE UNICORN DREAM

Douglas Hill

Illustrated by
D. S. ALDRIDGE

HEINEMANN · LONDON

Just for Kristyn
(sweet dreams)

William Heinemann Ltd
Michelin House
81 Fulham Road
London SW3 6RB

LONDON · MELBOURNE · AUCKLAND

First published 1992
Text © Douglas Hill 1992
Illustrations © D. S. Aldridge 1992
ISBN 0 434 97674 1

Produced by Mandarin
Printed in Hong Kong

A school pack of BANANA BOOKS 49-54 is
available from Heinemann Educational Books
ISBN 0 435 00108 6

Night Fright

BRIAN BROWN WAS a dreamer of
dreams.

In nearly every other way, he was a
fairly ordinary boy. He enjoyed most
things that boys enjoy – sports and
games, eating, running around making
lots of noise, watching television in the
evening. But he loved his dreams most
of all.

He never minded going to bed, because he knew that when he went to sleep he would have a dream. He didn't even mind the scary, bad dreams too much. In those dreams, when things got really frightening, he always woke up. Then he would lie there happily, knowing he was safe in his own bed, knowing it had been only a dream. Nothing to be afraid of. Nothing real.

At least, not until the night of the Unicorn Dream.

It was a lovely dream, at first. The unicorn was beautiful, a shiny silvery colour with a flowing white mane and tail. And of course with a long sharp horn jutting out of his forehead.

In the dream Brian rode the unicorn across meadows where every grass blade had a smiling face. And over a blue beach where the sea made big purple bubbles for

the unicorn to burst with his horn.

At last they went into a forest of trees shaped like letters and numbers, where they saw birds with tiny propellers on their beaks and chased a bright butterfly as large as a man.

But the chase led Brian and the unicorn deeper into the forest. And there the dream changed. Suddenly there were dark clouds above them and dark shadows around them. In the bushes Brian could hear a rustling, a padding of paws, a harsh breathing that was almost like growling.

Then the breathing became even more like growling. Something padded out of the shadows in front of them. It was the size of a very large bear – though it seemed more the shape of a very large dog.

And in the midst of its huge shadowy shape, Brian saw slanted green eyes, a

gaping scarlet mouth and long sharp
shiny teeth.

The monster's mouth opened wider.
The fangs glittered. From its throat came
a deep baying howl. Then the monster
leaped at Brian and the unicorn.

Brian tried to scream, but couldn't. He
felt the unicorn beneath him trying to
jump away . . .

And then Brian woke up, with a kick
and a jerk and a muffled cry.

A wonderful feeling of relief swept over him as the dream-horror faded away. He lay back on his pillow, feeling warm and safe.

Then he heard, there in his bedroom, a totally impossible sound. A sound like . . . *clop*. Like a hoof.

He sat up – and stared.

At the foot of his bed, staring back at him, stood the unicorn.

Dreamwhere

'DON'T LOOK SO surprised,' the unicorn said crossly. 'This is mostly your fault, you know.'

'What . . . how . . . where . . . ' Brian gabbled.

'After all, it was your dream,' the unicorn went on. 'You're the one who brought the Night-Hound into it. All very well for you. You can jump back to the real world, leaving me on the other side with the Hound. Well, no thanks. Not me. When you jumped back, I jumped with you.'

Brian blinked a few times. 'Am I still dreaming?'

The unicorn sighed. 'That's like asking someone if they're lying. This could be a dream in which I tell you you're not dreaming.' He shook his mane. 'Although the fact is, you *aren't*. This is real. Which means that I'm in trouble.'

Brian opened his mouth, but was unable to think of anything at all to say.

The unicorn went to look out of the window. It was very late, past the middle of the night, and everything was made

darker by heavy clouds and a drizzle of rain.

'Just what I don't need,' the unicorn said. 'Rotten weather, a boring town, and no one to help me but a little kid who can barely speak.'

That stung Brian. 'I'm not little – I'm nearly ten,' he said firmly. 'And I *can* speak. I just . . . I don't understand.'

The unicorn turned and looked at him for a long moment. 'All right,' he said at last. 'I'm just feeling bad-tempered. I suppose it *is* all fairly surprising. I'll explain while you get dressed.'

'Dressed?' Brian asked.

The unicorn waved his horn at the window. 'Out there in your town – I hope – is a way for me to get back to the Dreamwhere. I need to find it before sunrise, or I'm done for. So I need your help. So let's go!'

The last word was said sharply enough
to bring Brian quickly out of bed, reaching
for his clothes.

'Now then,' said the unicorn. 'We sort
of know each other, you and I. You've
dreamt of me before. I'm Cornelius. You
do not call me Corny, *ever*.'

Brian found that he was able to smile.
'All right. And I'm . . . '

'Brian,' said Cornelius. 'I know.

You're well known in the Dreamwhere. Most people just pop over for a minute or so, and never do much. But you're one of the special sort that have big, interesting dreams. Loads of fun.' He sighed. 'If you could just keep the monsters out.'

'I'm sorry,' Brian said. 'I didn't mean to dream that thing . . . What did you call it?'

'The Night-Hound,' Cornelius said. 'One of the worst monsters in the Dreamwhere.'

'What's the Dreamwhere?' Brian asked.

'The Somewhere you go to when you're dreaming, of course,' Cornelius told him. 'It's a place that's as big or small as a dream wants to be, filled with as many kinds of things as a dreamer can imagine. Including unicorns and monsters. Are you nearly ready?'

Brian nodded, tying his shoelaces.

'It's not really fair, you know,' Cornelius went on. 'You can cross over to the Dreamwhere any night with no risk of getting stuck there. But if we cross over to the real world and don't get back before sunrise . . . ' He drew a hoof across his throat in a very unpleasant fashion.

Brian swallowed. 'Why can't you just go back the same way you came?'

'I told you,' Cornelius said. 'I came with *you*, when you jumped back. That was *your* crossover place. Now you're awake, it isn't there any more. So I have to find a different crossover place. A special one.'

'What kind of special?' asked Brian.

'I need a special bridge,' the unicorn told him. 'One that crosses no water – and that has only one end. And with the moon shining on it.'

Brian's eyes were wide. 'But that's . . .

'Impossible,' said Cornelius
unhappily. 'I know. Especially the chance
of a moon on a night like this. But I have to
go out and look. And hope. There's a few
hours of darkness left. We might get
lucky.'

Searching

THEY LEFT THE house silently, except for a *clop* or two from Cornelius's hooves. They went along the street more silently, since Cornelius stayed on the grass verge where his hooves made less sound.

Cornelius trotted along quite quickly, looking around, and often Brian had to break into a run to keep up. It seemed that there would be no riding on the unicorn's back this time. So Brian began to get a bit out of breath. He was also getting wet from the steady drizzle. But he didn't mind. It showed him that he really *wasn't* dreaming. Never in any of his dreams had he ever felt cold or wet or out of breath.

Besides, everything in the town around him looked ordinary and normal and not

at all dream-like. Everything except the silvery unicorn trotting along ahead of him.

As they came to a big junction, Brian was puffing quite hard. But he was also smiling with happiness at how wonderful it was to be really out with a unicorn. His smile faded, though, when Cornelius stopped and looked at him.

'Right, then,' he said. 'Which way?'

Brian looked blank. 'I don't know.'

'Wonderful,' the unicorn said. 'Then tell me this. Does the town have a river going through it?'

'Yes,' Brian said, pointing. 'Over there.'

'Fine,' Cornelius said. 'We'll go the other way.'

Brian frowned, then remembered. Cornelius wanted to find a bridge that *didn't* cross water.

And with only one end. And with moonlight . . .

Shaking his head, he hurried away after the unicorn. On they went, searching the town – up streets and down avenues, along high roads and through narrow lanes. They saw many things in their search, but no one-ended bridges. And also, along the way, they were *seen*.

They were seen by cats who yowled and fled.

They were seen by dogs who barked wildly. Worst of all, they were seen by people. Brian had no idea there were so many people out so late at night.

The first one to see them was a hairy, scruffy tramp who had been sleeping in a doorway until he was awakened by the *clop* of unicorn hooves. He staggered to his feet and shouted 'Hoy!' and looked as if he wanted to follow them. But Brian and Cornelius whisked round a corner and away.

Then there was a milkman, on his heavily loaded float, who spotted them and shouted 'Hoy!' and tried to turn the float to come after them. But he turned too sharply, some milk crates fell off with a crash, and he had to stop and clear up the mess.

As Brian and Cornelius ran away from him, they almost ran straight into a police car. The two policemen inside it shouted 'Hoy!', turned on the car's flashing lights and came rushing up the street. But Brian and Cornelius were able to duck into a narrow passage between buildings. By the time the policemen were out of their car and puffing along the passage, the boy and the unicorn had run out of the other end, across a small park and safely away along another street.

That brought them into a part of town full of small factories and warehouses without many houses or shops. And there they were spotted by a night watchman, who shone his torch on them and shouted 'Hoy!' He might have chased them, too, if

he hadn't been inside a wire fence with a
locked gate.

'Cornelius, all those people *saw* you!'
Brian said worriedly, when they were out
of sight.

Cornelius tossed his head. 'Doesn't
matter. In the morning they'll all think
they were dreaming.'

He trotted on as quickly as ever. But
Brian still had no idea where to go next to

find the special dream-bridge that
Cornelius needed. And it looked as if part
of the sky was growing a little *lighter*,
behind the clouds.

Cornelius was looking at the sky too.
'Dawn isn't far away,' he said. 'And
sunrise comes soon after dawn. We have
to *hurry*. Can't you think of somewhere
to look?'

Brian sighed and tried to think. But
before any ideas could come to him, he
was startled out of his thoughts by a storm
of growling and barking from the
darkness behind them.

For a terrible moment Brian thought it was the monster from his dream that Cornelius called the Night-Hound. Then he realized that it was just some stray dogs barking, as before. Except that this time, the noise seemed to be getting closer.

'Quick!' Cornelius said. 'Those dogs are after *us*!'

They dashed away, Brian trying to make his weary legs keep up. Around a corner they swept, into a narrow

alleyway between two warehouses. Then Brian nearly crashed into Cornelius as he skidded to a stop.

The sky had grown light enough to show that the far end of the alley was blocked.

They were trapped.

Around the corner after them galloped the dogs – a half-wild pack, barking viciously.

The dogs stopped their wild rush when they saw Cornelius. Then they came forward slowly, crouching low, showing their teeth and growling horribly. Cornelius lowered his head, the dagger-sharp horn gleaming, and stamped on the ground with his sharp front hooves.

Suddenly the dogs stopped, tails between their legs, looking around nervously. All at once they turned and ran, out of the alley, at top speed.

'Certainly scared *them* off,' Cornelius said proudly.

But then they both found out what it was that had *really* frightened the dogs.

From not too far away they heard an eerie, blood-freezing, baying howl. A terrifying sound that Brian had heard before. In a dream.

The howl of the Night-Hound.

The Chase

'RUN!' CORNELIUS SHOUTED.

In a panic, Brian tried to follow as the unicorn sprang away. But tiredness and terror drained the last strength from his legs. He stumbled and almost fell as the Night-Hound howled once more, much closer.

Then, wonderfully, Cornelius was beside him again.

'Jump on, Brian!' Cornelius yelled. 'We'll give the Hound a race!'

Somehow Brian managed to fling himself on to the silvery back as Cornelius leaped away again. He found that riding a unicorn in real life wasn't as easy as in a dream. He bounced and jiggled and bumped and would have fallen off if he hadn't dug his fingers into the thick mane and hung on with all his might.

They fled out of the alleyway like a
flash of silver lightning. Behind them the
Night-Hound bayed again, but the
fearful sound faded as Cornelius's speed
took them away.

The narrow street that they were on led
them out of the town. Soon it became
wider, with trees instead of buildings, as it
became a highway out into the country.
And just then Brian realized that
something very odd was happening.

Cornelius was singing.

It was a tune without words, jaunty and

merry. Not at all how he should have been
feeling with the sky full of dawn and the
Night-Hound on their trail.

'What . . . ' Brian tried to say,
clinging to the mane.

Cornelius laughed. 'You think I've
gone crazy? No – I'm *happy*! The Night-
Hound's *here*, in the real world!'

'B-but . . . ' Brian stuttered.

'Don't you see?' Cornelius said. 'The
Hound didn't cross over with *us*, when
you jumped back out of your dream. If he
had, he would have been there in your

room when you woke up!'

That thought made Brian shiver and grip Cornelius's mane even harder.

'But since the Hound is here,' Cornelius went on, 'it means he found *another way*! A different crossover place!'

Brian gulped and understood.

'So there *is* a way!' Cornelius almost sang. 'There *is* a crossover place! And if we can find it in time, I can get back!'

'But the Hound . . . ' Brian said.

'Oh, he'll come after us, of course,' Cornelius said airily. Then he glanced back at Brian's white face. 'I mean after *me*. He can't hurt *you*, here in the real world. But he could tear me to pieces here or anywhere. So I have to stay ahead of him. And find the crossover place before he finds me.'

Brian shivered again. 'I wish I could

help,' he said in a small voice.

'Never mind,' Cornelius began. Then
he stopped. 'Look, Brian! Look *up*!'

Brian looked. He had known that the
sky had been getting brighter. But the
brightness wasn't all from the dawn.

The rain had stopped. The clouds were
drifting away, tearing apart like ragged
cloth. And in the western sky, quite low,
the torn clouds were letting through a soft
and silvery light.

The light of the moon, as it began to set.
But then Brian and Cornelius looked
the other way, towards the east, where
the grey glimmer of the dawn was tinged
with rosiness.

'The sun's coming up any moment,'
Cornelius said. 'And the moon's going
down. My time is running out, Brian. If
the sunlight touches me, I'm finished.'

Sunrise

ONCE AGAIN, BRIAN tried to think as hard as he could for an answer to the problem. But before anything came to him he heard, terrifyingly close behind them, the monstrous howl of the Night-Hound.

He looked round to see the huge dark monster bounding along the road behind them at a frightening speed.

Cornelius galloped wildly away. And Brian, clinging to his mane, frozen with fear, suddenly saw something ahead of them. Something he had seen before. It was a side road, curving off from the highway. And he had seen it before, Brian realized, because it was on the edge of town very close to his own home.

Somehow he and Cornelius had travelled through the town in a circle. And now, seeing the side road, Brian remembered . . .

'Up there!' he shrieked, pointing.

Cornelius leaped away, as the Night-Hound's terrible howl rose again behind them. The side road sloped up steeply, but Cornelius flashed up the slope like a bullet from a silvery gun. Then he stopped, at the top of the slope, with a cry of joy.

The side road led on towards a flyover being built above another roadway. And the flyover was a long way from being finished. It stretched out from the top of the slope – and came to an end.

In mid-air.

Reaching nothing, going nowhere.

There was even a swirl of early-morning mist around the far end of the flyover, as an extra dream-magical touch.

'That's *it*!' Cornelius cried. 'A bridge with one end, not over water! Perfect! And the moon too!'

He leaped towards the flyover in a blaze of speed. Looking back, Brian saw the Night-Hound racing along towards the bottom of the slope, deadly fangs glittering. And in the east, the redness of the sky started turning to fiery orange, as the sun began to rise.

Then Cornelius planted his hooves and slid to a stop on the very lip of the unfinished flyover. Brian tumbled from his back and found his feet as the unicorn

grinned at him.

'Thanks, Brian,' Cornelius said. 'I wouldn't have made it without you.'

'*Hurry*!' Brian gasped. 'It's *coming*!'

Cornelius nodded. He looked westward at the setting moon, and ahead at the mist around the end of the flyover. Then he simply jumped. Into the mist. Off the edge. Out of sight.

Brian stared into the mist, trying to see

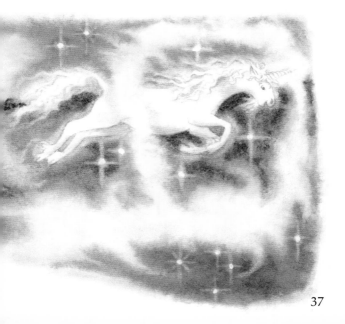

the silvery shape. But then he heard the raging howl behind him, and whirled.

The Night-Hound had reached the top of the slope. Its dark hugeness was outlined against the orange-red eastern sky. The green eyes blazed, the curved fangs flashed.

Brian shrank back, too frightened even to cry out. He wanted to run, but he couldn't. The Hound was ahead of him, the edges of the flyover were on either side. And behind him was the end of the flyover where Cornelius had gone.

Suddenly he felt icy-cold, thinking of what Cornelius had said could happen if the Hound followed the unicorn into the Dreamwhere. But at the same time Brian remembered what else Cornelius had said.

It can't hurt *me*, here in the real world, he said to himself.

All at once he wasn't afraid any more.

He braced himself, standing as tall as he could, fixing his gaze on the piercing green eyes of the approaching monster.

'Get back!' he shouted. 'I won't let you have him!'

To his amazement, the Hound skidded to a halt. It even backed away a step or two. Then it howled again and gathered itself for a mighty leap – a leap that would have taken it over Brian's head, on to the end of the flyover.

But in that moment the eastern sky suddenly turned dazzling gold. The sun had risen. Its rays reached out over the land like long golden arms of light. And some of the arms touched the Night-Hound.

The Hound howled in fear. But then the howl grew faint – and the huge shadowy shape began to fade away, disappearing into nothingness. The end of night had brought an end to all nightmare creatures, including the Hound.

Brian took a deep breath. All his terror had been washed away by the sunrise. As he set off for home, nearby, he felt only a little sad, wishing that there was some way that Cornelius could have stayed with him.

But then he heard a voice, very faint and distant, from behind him. The voice of Cornelius.

'Bye, Brian,' the voice said. 'See you in your dreams.'